THIS CANDLEWICK BOOK BELONGS TO:

_____

_____

_____

For Jermaine ~ T. C.

For my Nan ~ P. H.

First U.S. paperback edition 2008

The Library of Congress has cataloged the hardcover edition as follows:

Cooke, Trish.
Full, full, full of love / Trish Cooke ; illustrated by Paul Howard.
p.   cm.
Summary: For young Jay Jay, Sunday dinner at Gran's house is full of hugs and kisses,
tasty dishes, all kinds of fishes, happy faces, and love.
ISBN 978-0-7636-1851-3 (hardcover)
[1. Grandmothers — Fiction. 2. Dinners and dining — Fiction. 3. African Americans —
Fiction.] I. Howard, Paul, date, ill. II. Title.
PZ7.C77494 Fu 2003
[E]—dc21   2001043761

ISBN 978-0-7636-3883-2 (Candlewick paperback edition)
ISBN 978-0-7636-4899-2 (All About Books edition)

LEO 21 20
21 20

Printed in Heshan, Guangdong, China

This book was typeset in Block.
The illustrations were done in acrylic and pencil.

Candlewick Press
99 Dover Street
Somerville, Massachusetts 02144

visit us at www.candlewick.com

Full, Full, Full of LOVE

Trish Cooke

illustrated by

Paul Howard

CANDLEWICK PRESS

On Sunday, Mama took Jay Jay
to Grannie's house.
"I'll go get Dad," Mama said.
"I won't be long!

Gran is soft and warm and full,
full of hugs and kisses.
Kiss, kiss.
Hugs and cuddles.

Grannie was cooking.
The dinner smelled yummy.
"Is dinner ready, Gran?" asked Jay Jay.
But Gran shook her head.
"Dinner's not ready yet," she said.
"Come . . . let's put out the dishes."

Grannie's cupboard is always full,
full of colorful dishes.
Clink, clank.
Clatter, clatter.

But Jay Jay was hungry.

"Is dinner ready now?" he asked.

Gran shook her head.

"Dinner's not ready yet," she said.

"Come . . . let's feed the fish."

Grannie's fish tank is full,

full of all kinds of fishes.

Splash, splish.

Wiggle, wiggle.

But Jay Jay was hungry.
So Jay Jay asked again,
"Is dinner ready NOW, Gran?"
Gran shook her head.
"Dinner's not ready yet," she said.
"Come . . . let's . . ."
Then Jay Jay saw the candy tin.

Grannie's candy tin was full,
full up to the brim.
Tip, tip.
Struggle, juggle.

Gran said, "No!"
But seeing all that candy
had made Jay Jay even hungrier
than before.
So he asked again,
"Is dinner NEARLY ready, Gran?"
Gran shook her head.
"Dinner's not ready yet," she said.
"Come . . . let's look for the others."

So they looked out the window
and they waited, and waited.
Tick, tock.
Snuggle, cuddle.

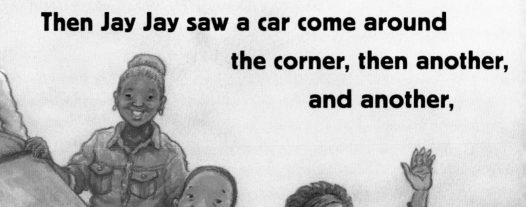

Then Jay Jay saw a car come around the corner, then another, and another,

and the cars stopped

           one behind the other.

                      And out they all came.

Uncles and aunties, cousins and friends,
Mama and Daddy.
All come for Sunday dinner at Grannie's!

"Dinner MUST be ready now, Gran!"
Jay Jay grinned. And Gran laughed.
"Mm-mmm, I think it is!"

There were
buttery peas,
chicken and yams,
macaroni and cheese,
potatoes
and ham.

Biscuits,
gravy,
collard greens,
pasta salad,
rice and red beans!
There was apple pie
and vanilla ice cream,
fresh peach cobbler
covered in steam,
raspberry sauce,
coffee and tea—
plenty, plenty for
everybody!

Jay Jay said, "I'm going to pop!"
And Cousin said, "I have to stop!"
"More pie please!" Uncle said,
and Auntie and Mama shook their heads.
"Not for me."
"I've had enough!"
Grannie let out a big belly laugh.
Dad said, "Just a little bit more!"
and on top of his cobbler
Gran started to pour
more raspberry sauce.

Everybody was full,
   full of Grannie's dinner!
   Yum, yum.
   Giggle, giggle.

Then Grannie pulled up a footstool,
put up her feet, and sighed,
"All right, you kids—
one wash, one dry!"

On Sunday, Jay Jay had dinner
at Grannie's house.
And when it was time to go,
he climbed on Grannie's lap.

He kissed her and she kissed him back.
And then they hugged
and hugged and hugged,
and full of hugs
they hugged some more.

Grannie's house is always full,
full of hugs and kisses,
full of tasty dishes,
full of all kinds of fishes,
full to the brim with happy faces,
full, full, full of love.

That's Sunday dinner at Grannie's house!

Trish Cooke is the author of numerous books for children, including the award-winning *So Much!*, illustrated by Helen Oxenbury. Of *Full, Full, Full of Love*, she says, "Sunday dinner is just another excuse for my family to party. And believe me, we do! On Sunday Mom's house is always full. It's like musical chairs sometimes because you can guarantee that if you get up from your chair, someone else will have filled it by the time you get back! The best thing is there are always lots of hugs to go around!"

Paul Howard has illustrated many books for young people, including *Look at You! A Baby Body Book* by Kathy Henderson, *Grandma's Bears* by Gina Wilson, and *Classic Poetry: An Illustrated Collection*, edited by Michael Rosen. Of *Full, Full, Full of Love*, he says, "Jay Jay's Sunday reminds me of my own nan's mammoth Sunday dinners when I was a child. From behind your shoulder Nan would always put more food on your plate — despite the helpless pleas, 'No more! No more!'"